LITTLE LOU AND JUST BEING YOU

Just Be You!! :)

Leslie Mitchell Assini

Leslie Mitchell Assini

Illustrations by Andy Yura

A CHARACTER PETS BOOK
A Division of LJM Communications

Book layout & formatting by Aaxel Author Services
ISBN: 979-8-218-30598-7

To My Family,
Thank you for reminding me to be myself.
I love you.

"Just be yourself and you will make friends."
-Clara, Age 7

"Don't hide yourself in glitter because glitter washes away."
- Abigail, Age 11

At the back of a pet store in tank number two,
swims a tiny, grey fish who is named Little Lou.
Lou dreams of one day becoming a pet.
But no one has picked her...well, at least not yet.

2

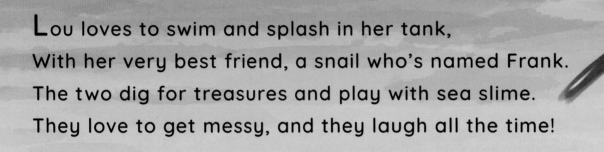

Lou loves to swim and splash in her tank,
With her very best friend, a snail who's named Frank.
The two dig for treasures and play with sea slime.
They love to get messy, and they laugh all the time!

4

One day while Lou makes a mud pie with Frank,
a new sign is put up outside of their tank.
"Look!" says Lou, "tomorrow's the pet fair!
It's our chance to be picked! Get ready! Prepare!"

6

Out of the blue, there appears a pink fish.
"Call me Priscilla," she says with a swish.
She flutters her fins and looks down at Lou.
"Poor thing!" she exclaims. "No one will pick you!
You're small and plain with that short, stubby tail.
You're messy and worse…your best friend is a snail!"

"How rude!" shouts Frank with a furious glare.
Lou watches Priscilla with an uncomfortable stare.

Priscilla sighs. "Just listen to me.
If you want to get picked, there are ways you must be!
The fish that get picked are the fanciest kind,
with glamorous fronts and gorgeous behinds!
Their scales have a sparkle, their fins are quite frilly.
They always look stylish, and never act silly!"

Be **dressy** (not messy)
Be **poofy** (not goofy)
Be **frilly** (not silly)
Be **shiny** (not slimy)
Be **slinky** (not stinky)

As Priscilla swims off, she shouts out to Lou,
"Take my advice! You know that it's true!"

Frank can see that his friend is upset.
"You're a great fish!" he says. "You'll be the best pet!"

Lou wipes a tear and says, "Frank, can't you see?
No one will want a plain, grey fish like me."
Right then, Lou decides she must be a new fish.
"I can't be myself if I want my pet wish."

The next day the pet store's the busiest yet.
Everyone's looking to find a new pet.

Lou's all dressed up, with glitter on her nose.
"ACHOO!" she sneezes as she strikes her best pose.

Lou thinks to herself, *This glitter makes me itch!*
I just want to squirm, scratch and twitch!

Even with all her glitter, most kids walk on by.
But Lou won't give up. There's more she can try!
She paints her grey scales a shimmery blue.
She covers her fins with seaweed, too.

But the paint is sticky, the seaweed weighs her down.
Will this even work? she wonders. *I feel like a clown!*

The last shopper leaves. The fair will soon close.
Lou is so sad and her frustration grows.
"Nobody picked me!" she says with a wail.
Then she sees something fuzzy that looks like…A SNAIL?

Lou looks again and sees Frank in a sweater!
He winks and asks Lou, "Does this make me look better?
I tried to be fancy, but I'm itchy instead!
This sweater's scratchy and I've got fuzz on my head!"

Lou bursts out laughing. "I feel silly, too!
I'm trying so hard to be someone new.
Although I'd love to be picked as a pet,
not being myself, I know I'd regret."

The two friends giggle and they both agree:
Being themselves is how they want to be!

One day while making some sloppy mud pies,
Lou hears a *tap tap* and gets quite a surprise!
A sweet, smiling girl is watching them play.
Lou's so excited! Will this be her big day?

24

25

The girl says, "I like the grey one, she's messy and fun.
Of all these tank fish, she's the happiest one."
The girl reaches in and scoops Lou in a net.
"I'll take the snail, too. He will make a great pet!"

"Hooray!" Lou cheers. "She picked you and me!"
"We're going to be pets!" They both giggle with glee.

"WAIT!" screams Priscilla. "This can't be true!
Why did the girl pick a grey fish like you?"
All the fish stop what they're doing and stare.
Then in a loud voice, Lou proudly declares:

28

"The answer is simple. It's because I AM ME. Just be yourself. It's the best way to be!"

About the Author

Leslie Mitchell Assini is a children's book author and communications professional based in Denver, Colorado. She lives with her husband, two daughters, a dog, a frog, ten fish, and a lizard. Leslie is the author of *Hungry Hudson Has a Choice*—the first book in the Character Pets series—inspired by real dogs, real friendships, and real birthday cake messes. *Little Lou and Just Being You*, featuring a lovable pet store fish, is her second book in the series.

Connect with Leslie:
@ @lesmitchellassinibooks   f @characterpetsbooks
www.lesliemitchellassini.com

About the Illustrator

Andy Yura is an illustrator based in Malang, Indonesia. Since 2018, he has been professionally illustrating children's books, bringing their stories and characters to life. Andy is soon-to-be-married and has a cat named Shiro.

Other Character Pets Books

Hudson is an adorable dog who loves his best friend, Ben.

He also loves food...a little too much!

When Hudson is faced with a decision that will show what kind of friend he is,

Hudson has a choice...

Will he make the right one?

Available through all major book retailers.

www.lesliemitchellassini.com

lesliemitchellassinibooks

Made in the USA
Monee, IL
20 April 2024